Tractor Saves the Day

Mandy Archer

Illustrated by Martha Lightfoot

QEB Publishing

The sun rises over the barnyard.

COCK-A-DO

Dog and Tractor are
wide awake already.

Good morning!

ODLE-DOO!

Dog opens the barn doors and pats
Tractor's **big, green hood.**

Dog **climbs** up Tractor's steps...
one, **two**, three.

BBRRRROOM!

He **sits** in the driver's cab
and **starts** the engine.

Tractor **chugs** down to the meadow.

Dog **jumps** out and opens the gate.

It's time to **feed** the cows!

Dog puts the **bale fork** onto Tractor. The big machine drives **backward**.

It **pushes** the fork into a hay bale...

...and **lifts** it into the feeder.

When they reach the top field,
Tractor **backs up** to the plow.

Tractor crosses **up** and **down** the muddy field.

The **plow** turns over the soil in furrows.

SQUELCH! CHURN! TURN!

Dog drives in neat, straight lines.

Tractor works hard until the field is done.
Tractor's **engine** needs to cool down!

Dog **unhooks** the
plow and stops
for a sandwich.

Dog looks up at the **blustery** sky.

The wheat field will be ready for harvesting. Time to move on!

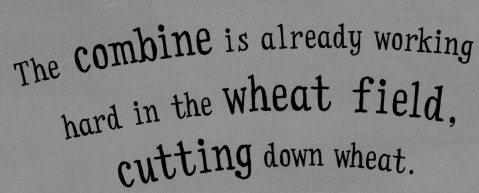

The **combine** is already working hard in the **wheat field**, **cutting** down wheat.

Dog **hooks** Tractor to its big, orange **baler**.

Tractor **chugs** along the **tracks** behind the combine.

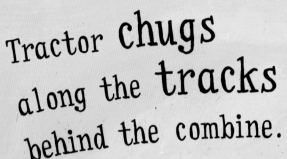

BRRROOM!

VROOM!

The baler picks up the **cut** wheat and **rolls** it together to make a bundle of straw.

At last the job is done.
Dog **unhooks** the baler.

HONK! HONK!

Tractor **turns** back toward the **barnyard**.

A **fallen** tree is
blocking
the path!

The wind has blown it down.

The tree **must**
be moved. The cows
need to get back to
the barn for **milking**.

The cows **watch** Tractor as Dog ties a **rope** around the tree, then **loops** it onto Tractor's **tow bar**.

Tractor revs its gears.

Its engine **shudders** and **Shakes**.

VROOOM!

Four big wheels dig into the mud.

The rope tightens as Tractor heaves and hauls the tree out of the way.

Tractor and Dog herd the **happy COWS** back to the milking shed.

Dog parks Tractor in the barn
and turns off its engine.

The sun sets over the barnyard.

It's been a good day's work!

Let's look at Tractor

Beacon

Driver's cab

Hood

Headlights

Wheels

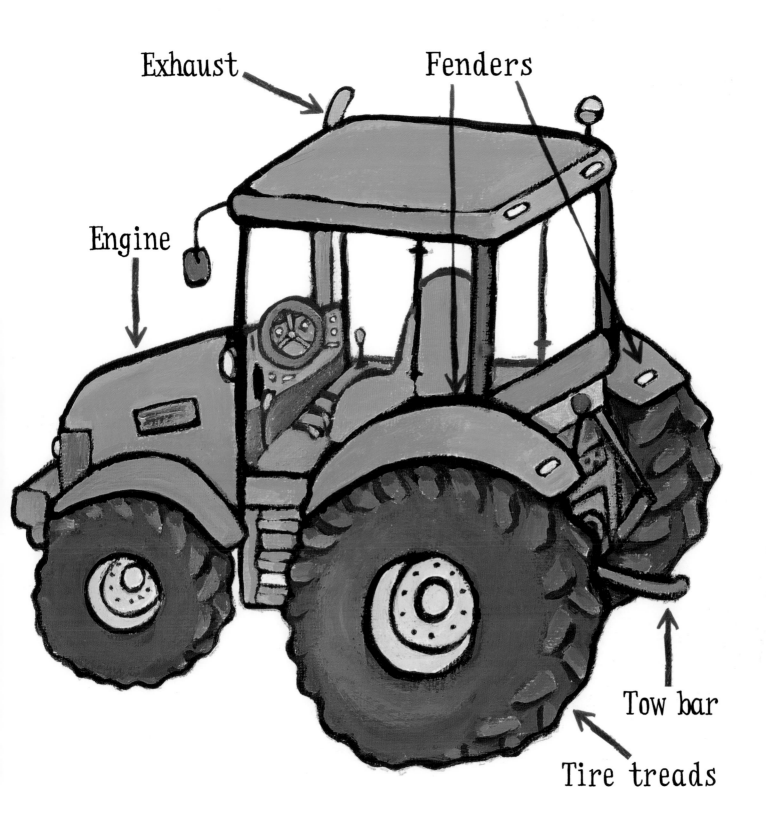

Exhaust

Fenders

Engine

Tow bar

Tire treads

Other Farm Machines

Combine

Baler

Plow

Crop sprayer

For Kitty, Olly, and Rosie M.L.

Designer: Plum Pudding Design

Copyright © QEB Publishing 2012

First published in the United States in 2012 by
QEB Publishing, Inc.
3 Wrigley, Suite A
Irvine, CA 92618

www.qed-publishing.co.uk

A CIP record for this book is available from the Library of Congress.

ISBN: 978 1 84835 821 8

Printed in China